Fissures

Fissures

[One Hundred 100-Word Stories]

GRANT FAULKNER

Press 53
Winston-Salem

Press 53, LLC
PO Box 30314
Winston-Salem, NC 27130

First Edition

Cover design by Patti Capaldi

Cover image Copyright © 2015 by Jamie Kingham,
licensed through Millennium Images, UK.

Author photo by Toby Burditt

Printed on acid-free paper
ISBN 978-1-941209-20-2

To my parents,
who made the world a creative place for me

Acknowledgments

The author wishes to thank the editors of the journals and magazines where the following stories first appeared:

365 Fiction, "Climbing"
Carve, "Extravagances," "Luna," and "Other Countries"
Connotation Press, "Departed," "Purposes," "Sacrilege," and "Souvenir"
The Cortland Review, "Filter"
Counterexample Poetics, "Castings," "Grey," and "The Tenderloin, 1997"
eclectica, "The Filmmaker: Eight Takes"
Fiction Southeast, "Charms" and "Infamy"
Flash Flood, "Dear X"
Flash International, "Heights," "Time Travel," and "Views"
Green Mountains Review, "Bodies at Risk in Motion," "Morphine Drip," "The Other Side," "Sophie's Dawn," and "The Toad"
Metazen, "Chiclets," "The Innocent," and "Decorations"
New Flash Fiction Review, "First Time"
PANK, "Model Upside Down on the Stairs"
Paragraph, "Abandoned," "Artifice," "Commemorations," "For the Love of Children," "Life on a String," and "Statue"
Puerto del Sol, "Blue Highways"
Revolver, "Life Knowledge"
Superstition Review, "Bright Mess"

Contents

Preface

The Spaces Boundaries Open Up

I've always thought life is more about what is unsaid than what is said. We live in odd gaps of silence, irremediable interstices that sometimes last forever. A lingering glance averted. The lover who slams the door and runs away. Unsent letters. We all carry so many strange little moments within us. Memory shuffles through random snapshots. Sometimes they seem insignificant, yet they stay with us for some reason, weaving the fabrics of our beings. In the end, we don't seize the day so much as it seizes us.

The idea of capturing such small but telling moments of life is what drew me to 100-word stories (or "drabbles" as they're sometimes referred to). I'd previously written novels and longer short stories, forms that demanded an accumulation of words—to sew connections, to explain, to build an entire world with text. I wondered, what if I did the opposite? What if instead of relying on the words of a story, I relied on the spectral spaces around those words? What if I privileged excision over any notion of comprehensiveness, and formed narratives around caesuras and crevices?

We live as foragers in many ways, after all, sniffing at hints, interpreting the tones of a person's voice, scrutinizing expressions, and then trying to put it all together into a collage of what we like to call truth. Whether it's the gulf between a loved one, the natural world, or God, we exist in lacunae. I wanted to write with an aesthetic that captured these "fissures," as I began to think about them.

Perhaps I could have accomplished such an aesthetic of writing in a longer form, but the hard borders of a 100-word story put a necessary pressure on each word, each sentence. In my initial forays into 100-word stories, my stories veered toward 150 words or more. I didn't see ways to cut or compress. I didn't see ways to make the nuances and gestures of language invite the reader in to create the story. But writing within the fixed lens of 100 words required me to discipline myself stringently. I had to question each word, to reckon with Flaubert's "mot juste" in a way that even most flash fiction doesn't. As a result, I discovered those mysterious, telling gaps that words tend to cover up.

We all have a literal blind spot in our eyes, where the optic nerve connects to the retina and there are no light-detecting cells. None of us will ever know the whole story, in other words. We can only collect a bag full of shards and try to piece them together. This collection is my bag full of shards.

Fissures

[One Hundred 100-Word Stories]

Castings

A resistance to spontaneous modes of imagination. A disdain for sultriness. Tattered underwear. Every marriage has its own legalities, and these were Anthony's claims for divorce. Sometime, long ago, they'd believed in something that rhymed with galactic. Now, if gossip columns about ordinary people existed, they would have reported him howling at the moon. In one last attempt to save their romance, he asked her to get high and lay on the grass. She held a grocery list, stared at him with a survivalist's determination. He saw teddy bears, grasshoppers in the clouds. The worms beneath him abandoned their selves.

Blue Highways

He often missed highway exits. Perhaps because he was dreamy, perhaps he just trusted that the road he was on would get him where he needed to be. He was surprised when he returned home one day and discovered his wife had left him. He called her cell phone, but she'd stopped her service. Her closet was empty, except for the dresses he'd given her. On the closet floor was a collage she'd made titled "The Places He'll Never Take Me." For her fortieth birthday, he'd put on a gaudy cape. He'd tried to pick her up in his arms.

Sophie's Dawn

Legs intertwined on a frayed pink Victorian couch. Her pale skin had grown paler, but Stockton didn't want to wake her. Dried leaves skittered on the windowpanes like guilty giggles. Her panties were still on, so they hadn't fucked. Tributaries of tiny blue veins lined her ankles, a strange map without towns. He covered her in a crocheted string-shawl. They'd written songs together around 4 a.m., and she'd shown him how to play flute on a bottle of Beam. "Who cares about a heart-healthy lifestyle," he joked. The moon soaked through his shoes. "You'll only be old once," she screamed.

Dear X

Dear X,
I loved you more than anyone could.
Love, Y

Dearest Y,
Funny. I didn't realize that. How are you?
Best, X

Dear X,
I cut my guts open for you. I'm bleeding.
Love, Y

Dearest Y,
Sorry to hear about the mishap. I hear there are remedies
for bleeding. Or it stops after a while.
Cheers, X

Dear X,
The bleeding won't stop. I'm split open.
Love, Y

Hey Y,
Can you believe this weather?
Yours, X

Dear X,
Why are you talking about the weather?
Love, Y

Dear Y,
I finally found the perfect beach!
xo, X

Model Upside Down on the Stairs

"A woman's beauty can be her damnation," her mother said. One guy told her he'd never seen an orifice he didn't like. Sure thing. But you've got to know something about tenderness. He just poked. She likes eyes on her, though, so she finds herself in the occasional awkward pose. Her boyfriend, the photographer. Her, the contortionist, the fucking astronaut. He'll have her hanging upside down from a tree tomorrow, his gaze going distant as his glory takes over. *Why doesn't anyone listen to me? Aren't ears an orifice?* The edges of the stairs wedged against her back. Never enough.

The Innocent

Zabeth placed the needle onto Siouxsie and the Banshees' "Spellbound" and slowly unbuttoned what she liked to call her "azul silk chemise," except it was polyester. Charley's eyes watched her just like the men in the peep show booth, except he stared into her eyes. One regular had lapsed in and out of consciousness today, his penis hanging limply from his trousers. The black light shined against the Day-glow oranges of a fluorescent cobra poster hanging over her bed. She unhooked her bra, dropped it to the floor. She watched Charley's eyes drift down, full of life, some might say.

Purposes

Celeste traced the swirl of cigarette smoke with her finger as it laced through the candy-colored globules of light from the lava lamps ringing her bed. As it disappeared, she wondered where it went. Particles dissipating beyond sight. She imagined Gerard picnicking with his family, lolling about on a summer day, his head in his wife's lap, but maybe he was dead now, hit by an RV in a grocery store parking lot. Last week she'd kissed her friend Chelsea, but now Chelsea lived in Amsterdam. She cupped her hand over the smoke to save it, then blew it away.

Souvenir

When Celeste thought of Gerard late at night, she emailed him tracks of yearning sexy songs. "Sorry to rape your ears," she wrote. She enjoyed thinking of her songs popping up on his iPod years later as he sat in his living room with his wife. "I love this song," his wife would say. "Where did you get it?" She imagined Gerard's eyes blinking, then gazing off into a memory of her, an ornery whiff of the past. True lovers are expert in constructing penitentiaries. She'd hammer a nail into his hands for eternity, even as she listened to static.

Life Knowledge

She searched for the perfect place to live. She changed her name from Clara to Claire. She drank one too many cups of coffee and then one too few. She painted porcelain dolls, then learned how to play the banjo. She made a promise in her diary never to get Botox. She asked, "Why do people hate the French?" She carried a pistol in her purse for protection, shampooed with anti-lice shampoo, just in case. She tossed breadcrumbs to golden carp and watched them mouth silent O's in the water. Poor things were too dumb to know anything about life.

Time Travel

"My life isn't some cheap reality show," he said to her when he left. It was 1979, years before reality shows even existed. He was like that, stepping in and out of time periods. When she first met him, he was wearing a top hat. Once he asked her to wear a garter for him on his birthday. She still had the garter. Yesterday, she tried to put it on, but her flesh wouldn't allow it after all these years. She'd had the crazy idea of surprising him, showing up at his offices at NASA, a vision from the past.

Heights

Robert was two inches taller than the tallest dwarf. It was like he was a species of his own. No girls wanted to slow dance with him in high school because his head would have rested on their breasts. Men clammed up when making dick jokes around him, although he thought his penis matched up well enough. Her name was Imelda. She was a masseuse in a dingy strip mall in El Cerrito. "When I got on the boat, they said I'd be a nanny," she said. He paid for extra time just so he could slow dance with her.

Filter

When Rex thought of Claudia, he felt like a cheerleader with Tourette Syndrome. Words exuberantly chased each other from his mind to his mouth, bounding and yelling with glee. The barbs of the tattoos on his biceps melted and dripped. His legs flexed, ready to jump. But then the words caught in his throat, choking him, too many sentences darting from too many different directions. To think he had once wanted to be a romantic crooner, a modern-day Dean Martin. He rested the telephone in its cradle. He put down his pen. He'd just have to hope that she knew.

The Other Side

The document posted on her door was written in an obscure language. The first time Maeve looked at it, she saw the words, "You owe me," but then there was a poem about a bee in the shape of a bee. She waited for ghosts to appear to translate. Insects filed under her door at night. *It's the uselessness of it all that is useful*, a husky voice whispered. The sound of ice in her grandmother's tumbler of rye. A body turned beside her in bed. She understood herself as vapor, larva in a bean, developing superpowers. Never before again.

Morphine Drip

"It's what we remember," Dad said, as if clinging to a frayed thread tossed to a man overboard in a storm.

He said something about a boy named Jim, his pants down to his ankles, his tuxedo shirt unbuttoned. Long baby hairs on smooth cheeks. Frogs croaking in the woods, gin rickeys under an August moon, the violet night. Outside a few parked cars, inside the ruckus of others.

"Never underestimate the comfort sin can provide," he said. "A lifetime of bedtime stories all to your lonesome."

Skin crinkled around his eyes. His dry lips pressed feebly around a straw.

The Tenderloin, 1997

The walls slobbered, the ceiling hovered, drooping close to Trevor's nose. His bedside lamp retched rays of light. Pink window shades, urine-yellow wallpaper. In the flowery dapples of sun on the carpet he tried to see the dance of a girl's smile. Two men spoke Russian in the next room. Funny how when Russians speak, it always sounds like someone is going to get killed. The desk clerk held no religious or medicinal powers. Just a witness of it all. Trevor's mother couldn't have guessed he'd sleep with a pistol under his pillow. Everything starts as a game of pretend.

Sacrilege

Celeste slowly ripped the collage Gerard had given her. She ripped through a woman's bodice, a faded lotto ticket, gold sprinkles becoming unmoored from the black paper and floating to the ground. She plucked off the dainty pink feather and twisted it in her fingers. If he was standing at the doorway watching her, his lips would squirm like a little boy holding back tears. If she had a whip, she'd snap it on the paper to see if it would bleed. She climbed into her bed and reached into her panties. *Lambent tongues of fire*, he'd written to her.

Departed

Celeste stuffed bags in overhead compartments, learned how to say "shower" and "bathroom" in other languages. Another apprenticeship with distance. Rio de Janeiro. Paris. Bangkok. She fucked an Australian on the beach in Phuket, made out with a man named Henri in the bathroom at Le Baron. Traveling through others' flesh was like smelling the air of exotic places. When she returned, she half expected to see Gerard waiting for her at baggage claim. He was watching her from somewhere, his elbow brushing against hers. She traveled in search of amnesia, but she'd only taken a Quaalude in the end.

Bright Mess

Z. lived in a boxcar that resembled a fairyland. Scarves, buttons, burn marks on the velvet of an armchair. Her nose, a hawk's. Her eyes, swirls of shining ice. Her arms, rubber bands. Most people didn't know how good she was with a yo-yo. As a child she wanted to be a mortician. As an adult, she wanted to be a clown, a puppeteer. *Memento mori*. We found her clutching a French crucifix. Thirty-four pills and a bottle of rum. Sketches of clouds wearing taffeta dresses adorned the ceiling. On one wall, she'd scratched, "You can't learn how to skip."

Chiclets

Gloria sometimes wondered if she was contributing to the ruination of married men. Tiny gold promises wrapped around fingers. The exchange of glances was so easy to understand that it always surprised her when men failed to comprehend the arithmetic. $2 + 2 = 4$. Follow me. Fuck me. Leave. Forever. Attending weddings was farcical. She wanted to stand at the lectern and tell the story of the man at the rest stop who stepped into a stall with her as his family waited in the station wagon, and then asked for change so he could buy his daughter gum.

Gray

Wendy wore a sleeveless dress split vertically down the middle, black on one side and white on the other side. We smoked Marlboros in my parents' basement while waiting for Mark, her boyfriend, my friend, to get off work. Then we'd all go get drunk together. I was the guy with the car, the guy with the six-pack. She dangled a high-heeled shoe on her foot, rolled her head back, exhaled smoke with a dazed pucker, and said, "Let's fuck." I stayed on the white side, an honorable fool, pondering it all as they made out in my back seat.

The Toad

Flattened by a car, its arms spread out, a little like Jesus. The sun had baked it as crisp as a potato chip.

"Poor toad," Maria said. "Didn't know how to cross the road."

"Maybe he thought the car was a new friend," I said. "Rushing to greet him."

"Or he was puzzling how such a small thing in the distance could become so large."

We spent hours in such conversations. It was nice, how we never talked about what was next, who we were together. As if the toad wasn't part of every story, in its way, even ours.

Luna

The nickname Cornflake wasn't exactly complimentary. He didn't know who'd tagged him with it, but it had stuck since the fifth grade. Hard to get dates when you're called Cornflake. He wrote poems about the moon—*la lune*, he called it—and folded them into Dolores's math textbook. Their legs brushed once, and he spent years wondering if she'd brushed her knee against his on purpose. He told people to call him Frosted Flake, but they called him Cheetos instead. Years passed. He wrote Dolores from Afghanistan. Did she ever find those poems? The moon here, wrapped in burlap. *Baddur.*

Other Countries

Randall told Abigail she looked French. Her dark eyes, the way she held a cigarette, the slender fit of her hips in a skirt. "It's silly to say, but you have a certain *je ne sais quoi.*" Later she'd think it was just a line: if you tell a woman she looks French, she'll remember you forever. He was so American that way, playing with all of the world's cultures, making them into a sales pitch. "You look like you're from Oklahoma," she told him. But, no, he was really just a little boy wearing his father's cowboy boots, tripping.

Extravagances

Frank hadn't bought a pair of pajamas in twenty-three years. He'd never eaten a rutabaga, or even tasted chocolate mousse, let alone sipped champagne. He'd always wanted to take tap dancing lessons, but tap wasn't pertinent in this age, Fred Astaire's footwork akin to Shakespeare's iambic pentameter. He nailed a board over the broken window in his bedroom and put an extra blanket on the bed. An old man deserved to be cozy, especially if no one lay beside him. Cary Grant always wore silk pajamas. Frank dreamed of a simple flannel nightshirt. He held Kim Novak in his arms.

Infamy

"When you're fat, it doesn't matter what you wear," Ginny said. "Nothing's going to cover up your blubber." She'd worn tight-fitting clothing and loose-fitting clothing, blacks and browns, stripes and plaids. That July morning, never to be forgotten, she walked through the town square "buck naked," as Ralph Wyatt told it. She felt the sun on each cell of her body and gloried in the sweat glistening on her arms. She hadn't gone barefoot since she was a girl. Men's eyes followed her as if she were a beauty queen, so she waved with a gentle twist of her wrist.

Charms

The sound of quarters dropping into the washing machine at the Laundromat. Things would be clean. The click of my mother's pocketbook opening. Things would be paid for. She tossed her purse into the front seat. We traveled. A man in a midnight suit, starched shirt, narrow black tie. He patted me on the head and took a dollar from my wallet. Dinah Washington's voice on the jukebox didn't soothe. Mom wanted to buy painted scarves from museum gift shops. Her hand gripped the faux crocodile handle of her luggage. Mechanics can never be charmed, but at least she tried.

For the Love of Children

After he had children, Gerard saw each person as another's son or daughter. The pinch of worry in a mother's eyes just after midnight. The dreadful wait until the front door creaked open once again. Safety. Or was it? He wanted to tell Celeste he touched her with such care, even as they lay in the strewn sheets of another cheap hotel room. He'd asked a friend to watch his children to be with her. Right then they might be crossing a street without anyone holding their hands. *Will you tie my hands behind my back?* He did so gently.

The Second Hand

Celeste wore a longing for death tightly across her forehead. She knew that each of their acts, no matter how distant in the mind, ended in a kind of murder or its kissing cousin, suicide. *I trust you like a wolf I raised from a pup*, Gerard said. In his arms she felt as if she lived on the equator, every hour motionless, vast, hot. The clock ticked on timelessness, except it didn't. She made sure to say she had to go before he did. She trusted him like a cardinal trusts a blue jay. *I'm a robin*, he said.

Undergarments

They were the type of people who always wore fine shoes. Shoes that looked as if they had just gone shoe shopping. They'd once prided themselves on having equally fine underwear. "Once you wear silk boxers, you can never go back," he used to say. She bought the finest lingerie, bras and panties of every kind, as if she were a collector. Now, however, as he folded the laundry, he noticed frayed elastic. The frilliness of her panties had become unfrilled. Tiny holes punctured the seams like paint chipping off the wall. One's undergarments are always the first to go.

Priceless Objects

"I've never made love to a black woman," he said. LaSandra should have been affronted to be categorized so, but how can one not like being exotic in another's eyes? He'd think of her as *the black woman* for the rest of his life.

He treated her as a museum piece. He studied her nipples like a scientist.

"I wish you were from Egypt, with a gold headdress," he said.

She traced the craggy lines that splintered from his softening eyes. Truth be told, she'd never slept with such an older man.

"Was his skin scratchy?" her best friend asked.

Fool's Gold

I used to be able to walk into a bar and fall hopelessly in love
with a woman. Any night, it didn't matter, there was always
a woman. I would sit at the bar, watch her talk to friends,
dance, and I'd love her until closing time. Then I'd walk
home on the lonely, dark streets remembering passed
glances, mysterious eyes that held worlds, and I might cry,
drunk, thinking of the road trips we didn't take, our children,
a dog. That was Chicago. 1989. It wasn't so bad to be a fool.
Wise now, I stay home most nights.

Decorations

Zabeth stopped dancing halfway into a pivot. Shaded dancers lifted their legs in the suspended cages around her, slinking anorexic bodies, sinuous beats. Tattoos flared and dissolved in the flickering lights. A heart, a feather, a dagger, lips and fingernails painted black. It was as if they were stranded in reckless elegance, cardboard cutouts of decadence above the crowd. We all need someone to see who we are, she thought. *Wistful mouth*, the manager said. *Excited tail.* She looked below her, but no one looked up. She needed to pee, and swayed her thighs as urine trickled down her leg.

Enough

I never got to kiss you in the middle of the Sahara, desperate sweat streaming down our faces. I never got to kiss you in a tent, swimming in a forest's darkness. I never got to kiss you in the produce section of a grocery store, or on a train going to Moscow. I never got to kiss you in the ocean, our bodies floating with the waves. I never got to kiss you in a casino, not even in a nightclub, not even on a Sunday afternoon. I only got to kiss you. I only got to kiss you.

Slicing

She organized her life into pie charts. He planned each moment according to something like Jackson Pollock drips. She saw allocations, all of life's arc in the curve of each slice. He traced his finger over the twists of bumpy paint, reckless sinews of anguish and glee dashing into eternity.

"I'll love you forever," he said.

"I'm done with my pie," she said.

There was cherry on her lips. He stared at it like a sign from heaven, but she licked it away as if wiping a counter. Her next slice would be bigger, no doubt, and topped with cream.

Life on a String

Celeste told him not to toy with her. But then Gerard found himself a yo-yo on her string. He asked questions. She told him nothing.

"But we fucked," he said.

"You called it making love."

"But you said it was fucking."

Up and down. She snapped her gum as she did yo-yo tricks: reaching for the moon, hopping the fence, punching bag. He was so dizzy, the whirr of the string tingling in his ears. But then everything stopped, and she cradled him in her soft hands. To ask why was futile. Why not? she'd say with a casual flick.

Vistas

What they had thought was safety. The smell of fresh espresso, a waiter's black shoe perfunctorily hitting the floor, the hotel's white towels. Gerard knew something she didn't, the way age exhausts the body. Celeste knew something he didn't, she was only half there. Snapshots. Her mouth would find another lover's just hours later. Tomorrow, a doctor would stick his finger up Gerard's ass to check his prostate. She put his presents into a shoebox and placed it next to her last boyfriend's. His wife's lips, terse now, difficult to kiss. Soon they didn't even know how to say hello.

Offerings

Tom's dad wheeled up in his silver Ford LTD, a tumbler of scotch on the dashboard, a cigarette in hand. He didn't get out, just rolled down the window and yelled, "Get in." He spoke in growls, grunts, sons-of-bitches. I never saw him without smoke trailing out his nostrils until later, when he drove a scooter carrying an oxygen tank. His wife fucked the golf pro, moved to Peoria. He got fired from the bank, had to return the LTD. Every Sunday, he took offerings at church. Somewhere in his razor-thin smile, I could tell he was flipping off God.

The Artist

A galumphing stride. A hacking cough. Wings of tangled hair flared from his eyebrows. Each morning "Old Frank" put a flower, a tussle of grass, a piece of pink plastic, something, in his lapel's buttonhole. His version of dignity. He drank grape soda out of a can with a straw. He painted pictures with ketchup in a booth at McDonald's. "My mamma told me I'd be an artist someday," he told the boy who stole his hat, then pushed him down. Grape soda streamed into the cracks of the sidewalk, glimmers of sunlight, splotches of red. His version of peace.

Matter

"Most things don't matter." That was the name of Rupert's company, which sold bumper stickers by the same name. Only his mother and ex-girlfriend Patty bought them, however, so he filled a room of his apartment with back stock. Each day he'd go out and stick one on a telephone pole, a car, a stop sign. Later, there was a punk band by the same name, then a sitcom, and finally a book by a Buddhist guru. "I came up with it all, and I didn't get any credit," he complained to Patty. She tucked her sticker into his casket.

Powers

Superman's penis hurt when he peed. A burning sensation at the tip. It felt worse than touching kryptonite, in a way. Sometimes he leaked. He'd gone through the usual battery of tests: a humiliating prostate exam, a scope twisted in his urethra, every sort of blood sample. To think that a man who had saved the world numerous times and would save it numerous times again was devoid of mojo in his loins, could never ejaculate without feeling a flatulent torque of his innards. No more lover boy. "It happens sometimes," was all his doctor could say. "Even to superheroes."

Flight

Bernard ran his fingers over the cigar burn on the table from long ago. The visible rarely shows what is important. To love another's restlessness is a definition of doom.

"I'm holding on upside down," he'd told George.

"Your mind resembles your grandmother's attic," George replied. "You're immersed in fussbudgetry."

Years later, he heard George cut off his right hand in a fever of religious delusion. Letters never sent. Bernard had always admired the ostrich. Why it chose not to fly, no one knew. A rebel bird, or perhaps just scared, like a boy refusing to jump into the pool.

Lips Meeting

The Pruitts gave Eugene his first soda, a Mountain Dew, when he was three. He sipped it from a straw in the smoky haze of their kitchen. His first beer, at the drive-in, made his face tingle to a chorus from the heavens. He'd always need something on his lips after that. Kisses appeared like mad laughing clowns in dreams, dashing away. The taste of gunmetal, the smell of plastic burning. When his veins cleared, he got high. The eternal question: to be with versus to be without? If he wouldn't have gone to the Pruitts', his mother always said.

The Filmmaker: Eight Takes

Take One: Above Ground

Alexander walked with the slovenly grandiosity particular to an underground filmmaker, his body at once large and commanding, soft and round. Puffy eyes. Grizzled disregard. If he'd stayed married to Victoria, his first wife, she would've buttoned up his shirt before his lecture, told him no one wanted to see wiry hair on an old man's chest. She lived by a lake now, sold ceramics, baked pies. "I'm making a film about India's brothels," he told her. "Sounds adventurous," she said, rolling her eyes as she turned away. To think, when she met him, he was scared of the dark.

Take Two: Always a Gentleman

Anisa lifted her legs around Alexander's waist, feeling the pinch of a broom against her back. He liked to fuck before public appearances; it gave him confidence. They found a closet in the basement. He was just three years younger than her father. If they met, they'd joust, two drunken peacocks. "I was a prince and you were a princess a thousand years ago," he whispered. His gravelly baritone, his asynchronous heartbeats. He pranced onstage that night, indulged in his burly wisdom like a prizefighter flexing his muscles. When he went on location, he always sent her flowers. *Love forever.*

Take Three: The Aspirant

"I don't believe in harmony. When I see a window, I want to kick it." Cole squinted his eyes tightly, staring at Alexander Van Seultan as if shooting bullets. He listened to his every word, however, even as he fixed on the gold chain around his neck. Van Seultan had probably worn tie-dye shirts in the 60s, danced in ridiculous twirls to the Grateful Dead. That was when you could be a pure artist, when movie theaters were palaces, not the cornerstones of strip malls. At a party later, Cole would say to a girl, "I don't believe in harmony."

Take Four: Cocksam

John Chang remembered Alexander opening the door to a massage parlor in the Tenderloin the first time he interviewed him. Asian darlings sashayed under a tattered disco ball, incense mixing with disinfectant in the air. "You wan' full body massage?" the old mamasan asked. He waited in the candy-colored shadows of the front room, imagining Alexander's whinnying red cock spitting at the girls. The mamasan gave him an orange. Now he and Alexander sat on stage, staring into a sea of furrowed brows. "I'm fascinated by relationships of power and labor," Alexander told him. "That's what my movies are about."

Take Five: Caring

Jimmy Lee could never tell what these artists were talking about. They fancified themselves in their learnings, spoke in tongues. This motherfucker talked all about exploitation, but peed on the damn restroom floor and didn't wipe it up. "Your boots are cool," the filmmaker exclaimed later, flinging back strands of hair. "Where did you get them?" Work boots. Buy 'em at the work clothes store. Someone spilled wine on the carpet at the reception. Another forgot his black leather coat on the rack. The only thing Jimmy Lee knew about these people was that they needed to be cared for.

Take Six: Swelling

"Did you ever have sex with the prostitutes you filmed?" an audience member asked. The worst thing about aging was how it voided desire. Alexander's dick burned when he peed now. Women were museum pieces, nothing more. He gazed out into the crowd, spotted a moping undergrad. Unwashed hair, a safety pin fastened in her nose. In another era, he would have smiled at her. She would have taken him to an after-hours party. *Her body draped over a sink, his hands upon her waist.* The physical and existential shouldn't mix with the sacred. He winked at her. He waited.

Take Seven: Coverings

"Women look most beautiful clothed," Alexander told Rachana, so she only undressed to her bra and panties. He looked funny, his bulbous stomach hanging over tight bikini underwear. She lay her head on his chest, told him stories, no sex. He paid $100, far more than her other clients in Delhi. No payment for going on stage tonight, though. People's eyes clawed at her, worse than any man. She stole a bottle of wine from the reception, took Alexander's car keys. "I'm in America," she screamed. Her mother would say she was free. Her grandmother would say she was lost.

Take Eight: Battles

Vladimir never tired of staring at rain-slicked streets. He drove his cab as if following keening, iridescent voices in puddles, smoking Sobranies, sipping Stoli, so he didn't listen to the drunken man in the backseat. "An artist's bravery is like a soldier's," the man bellowed. "The dangers of your soul are like a battlefield." When Vladimir pulled up to the hotel, the man was asleep, saliva curdling at the side of his mouth, shirt unbuttoned to his stomach. There was only $80 in his wallet, a creased photo of him with a woman, both of them in tie-dye shirts, dancing.

Artifice

"Museum guards are the most enlightened people on the planet," Celeste said.

"But they always look bored."

"Perhaps they're beyond the realm of passions."

Gerard thought of the guards later as they lay in bed in the dimming light of a hotel room just down the street from the art museum. The guards stared impassively into space, no matter the wild thrusts of the art around them. They waited, kept watch, much like he'd wait later that evening with his wife in the chaotic clatter of their house. Colors went unnoted. He was there only to make sure nothing broke.

Statue

Celeste was surrounded in the restaurant by her friends, titters and cackles of laughter. She'd sent them his emails, his love letters. Snarky online jokes carried over to brunch the next morning. One called him a fool. Another called him a stalker. Gerard saw himself as just another great artist in the Romantic tradition. He drew a picture of the statue that should be erected in his honor: the man who tried to say everything in his heart. A pigeon perched on his head, shat, and then flew off. Two lovers walked by, but they didn't notice him. For eternity.

Vive la Résistance

It was 1985. I dropped out of college and bought a plane ticket to Paris, where I found the last remnants of the Resistance living in the Latin Quarter. Old men, wrinkles like crevices, proudly smoking cigarettes in a garret strewn with empty wine bottles. No one needed sleep. They discussed the fabrication of gold and its metaphysical implications. Why alchemy? I asked. Once you taste a good battle, it's impossible to stop, they told me. A knife stuck in the wall. A Bible sat on top of a *Playboy* magazine in the bathroom. They'd run out of toilet paper.

The Scar

The good thing about having a scar on your face is you've always got a story to tell, Henry said. Brianna planted tiny bourbon kisses around the scar as if her lips could heal. Mathilde traced it with her finger, an archaeologist of hurt. Tavi just stared at it. Henry liked to say he got the scar when he was a pirate, a bank robber, a boxer. It was just an ordinary summer day, though, his parents arguing like hopped-up mosquitoes. A razor blade, time to kill. None of us are born to tie knots, but most of us do.

The Icing

Martin remembered when he and Delia breathed each other in, telling and retelling their stories. Waking up took hours, a time of life that now seemed as far away as playing with blocks in preschool. He yearned to run away—anywhere, really—yet he found comfort in their listless love. A good loaf of bread. Butter. Simple familiarity can be salvation. That's what they don't tell you when they point to the bride and groom on a wedding cake and say, "That will be you someday." The couch hurt his back, but he liked hearing her sleep in the bedroom.

Just Another Song
about Los Angeles

Desmond wrote songs about leaving Los Angeles. He was broke. His apartment cost too much. His girlfriend had dumped him. All of his friends were making movies, scheduling lunches, going to fundraisers. Each day he began to pack his car, but then a song would come to him. He called it a life of subsistence, music as food, religion as leaving, then staying. La Cienega. Palm trees swayed like drugged witches over changing billboards. Jigsaw puzzles of cars, endless freeway loops. *Are we gonna make it?* If Los Angeles were a woman, a judge would've given him a restraining order.

Nostrums

I've forgotten what I forgot this morning. Too much, or too little (it's always difficult to know), of my favorite nostrum: Kickapoo Indian Sagura. A nostrum to help me find the right nostrum. The skin is a glove that wrinkles as it tightens. If I were a good citizen, I'd join the crowd, seething in its clarity, fingers pointing in herky-jerky insistence. But I prefer to sit and wait to remember. Someday someone will bring me tea with a little pewter spoon, sugar cubes, cream. I'll point to my transistor radio, say turn it on. That's how you hear extraterrestrials.

Hammering

It was just one lovely September day, Gerard wrote. A silhouette, a shape, a mood. You should have asked me about the benefits of restrained desire. I glorified myself for having chosen you, perfect in your imperfections. My language fumbled; you chose not to speak. I said you were adorable, the way you sat in a chair. You said you wanted to fuck me. Your image out of thousands suited my desire. What an odd way to say such a thing. *Adorable* doesn't mean much, though, does it? And then fucking made it not so. A hammer on a butterfly.

Commemorations

One never leaves some places behind. The billowing white curtains of the hotel room in Anaheim, fireworks shooting over the enchanted castle. "Can you believe we fucked in Disneyland?" Celeste said. In Boston, she slipped a note under the door. "May this not be about regret, but joy and wisdom." He could still remember the wedge of morning light striking the carpet so timorously. They dined on room service in Dallas, showered together in Atlanta. They deserved a plaque outside of each room. He saw only the hallways now, the maids' carts full of clean towels, soap. Other people's rooms.

Views

Ron was the type of man who washed his windshield every time he filled his car with gas. He'd never pondered the word *grace*, even though he went to church each Sunday. He'd sung the word thousands of times in the choir, intoned the word with religiosity. He would only think of grace later, reflecting on the moment he told the police he hadn't done anything wrong. He stared at a bug smashed against his windshield. Felipe lifted his head from his lap, his hair mussed. The policeman's eyes bore into him like a drill. Felipe's drifting gaze, an angel's.

Dulcet

Succotash. Rutabaga. Wonderful words. Absinthe. Diaphanous. Ingénue. Even pamplemousse. I can say these words over and over on a dreamy Saturday morning, as if caressing a lover's breast. Lissome. Pastiche. Evanescent. Snails think of such words as they slither so slowly on their way, absorbing the sumptuous wafts of scents in the air. They feel each of their movements as lithe, graceful. Desuetude. Flaneur. Insouciance. Patina. Why don't people think of snails as great lovers, masters of sensuality as they mellifluously dream of ratatouille, rushing in their way to find it? We should follow the ephemeral gossamer of their trail.

What the Rooster Tells You

Ian bristled at the word *strategy*, a word that implied a way to figure out the world, conquer it. Corporate conference rooms weren't designed to recognize such nuances, though. It was like trying to write poetry in an Excel spreadsheet. So he doodled his way through another meeting, tallying the number of times people said "strategy," "synergy," "robust," daydreaming about his father sitting on a stool at the Red Rooster bar in his hometown. "Sometimes the best strategy is not to have one," he said. He was a man who lived too much in theory, Ian's mother liked to say.

Drinking Martinis in Jelly Jars

"Yooo hooo, yooo hooo," Margery called, her voice ringing through the spruces, as if a runaway dog answered to such a call. George asked himself what call he answered to. The dog, Beau, had dashed off after another dog. They'd gotten him at the pound, last year's Christmas present. "Yooo hooo," Margery sang. Just last night they'd boiled lobsters over a driftwood fire on the rocks. George dozed on the sofa listening to Vivaldi. Rain on the roof at 4 a.m. He counted the women he'd kissed in his lifetime. Twenty-three. Never enough. Go Beau, he said under his breath.

Vapors

Barbituate thoughts traipsed through his head like an ancient centipede picking up one leg at a time. Sunlight fringed the door, a taunt. All the air held an annoying menthol crispness, as if he'd fallen into a container of Vick's VapoRub. Tara scrubbed the kitchen counter, using three different kinds of disinfectant, just to be sure.

"I read some germs are good for you," he said. "Imagine that. A world with good germs."

She cried when the elastic of her underwear stretched out. She cursed the wind for bending trees. She scratched a pimple on her cheek until it bled.

After the Scream

No one had time to clean up the scary stuff. No, we're not talking about the empty wine bottles that filled the recycling container, the bottle of Courvoisier with a sliver of cognac at the bottom. Men who live for adventure never stop living for adventure, even if they go to work each day as diligently as an ant. Frayed strands of fake cobwebs from Halloween hung across bushes in the front yard. The box of the kids' costumes was overturned. The Scream mask was missing. He wasn't home in time for church the next morning. The silence was lovely.

Floating

A giggle passed over Lizzie's face as she stepped off the ledge. Later I'd think how odd it was that she pinched her nose with her fingers. The same nose that sniffed the glue in our slum cocktail, which doubled as her sixteenth birthday cake, the plastic bag billowing in and out in the bliss of fumes. After she hit the water, her giggle turned into a garbled scream, the rush of the current sucking her under like a monster grabbing her. Each time we jump now, we pinch our noses. None of us can explain the joy of falling.

Way Station

In Puerto Umbria, Maeve rented a room from a whorish-looking landlady. There was no door, only a wispy pink curtain. Her giggling brood of daughters kept slinking in to watch her dress and brush her teeth. There was little else to do than drink each night. A feline-looking boy in front of the cantina put his arm around Maeve and said, "Come in and have a drink," letting his hand slip down to her ass. Vultures ate a dead pig in the muddy street. She found comfort in the pink lamp's dirty tassels. Sometimes any kind of touch felt good.

The Truth

It doesn't exist, of course. Some say, "But the affair," as if such a thing can be placed antiseptically on a microscope slide. My grandfather told me tales of other lands. Mist clinging to treetops, gentle drips of moisture falling with whispers. Ghosts reside in the pearly swirls, he said, tragic lovers who just can't leave. Absences can move with such a force. What's gone is more important than the study of mass and volume. There's always the question, "Who was she?" I tried to memorize the curve of her lips. It seemed like a simple enough thing to do.

Abandoned

Each winter, as Gerard sat outside and watched his hands purple in the cold, he chastised Celeste for her selfishness. But it's always difficult to know who abandoned whom.

"I can't leave my family," he said.

"I can't forfeit myself," she said.

Now she sat alone in the penumbra of a party's flitting lights, damning him. He wrote letters he never sent. She sketched his torso in the middle of the night. He bought a cupcake on her birthday. She kissed a man who looked just like him. I'm Romeo, he told a dog. I'm Juliet, she told a snake.

Making Music

No one heard that last faint guitar twang from Charley Dare's studio apartment on Shotwell and Capp. San Francisco. The Mission. December 26, 1991. THE LAST GREAT ROCK 'N' ROLL SONG was spray-painted in red on the sidewalk. If his parents would have listened to the cassette tapes they found when they cleaned out his apartment, they could have heard the song. "One, two, three, four," sung over and over to layers of grizzled guitar chords. Crescendos. Diminuendos. A sharp yell, a dangling whisper. "Five, six, seven, eight." And then that single lonely twang looking for something to cling to.

Bodies at Risk in Motion

As he undid his belt, his erection snuck over the top of his white underwear. Zabeth saw his khaki-colored life fade away, the man of rules breaking the rules. A shopping mall bathroom. She looked at his gold wedding ring, wondering if he was there with his family, a teenage daughter. He cupped her buttocks, fingers searching. She noticed a tiny scar by his left eye, a story she'd never hear. He pressed his chin down, appearing to be in pain. "I should leave first," he said. She adjusted her panties, knowing better than to look in the bathroom mirror.

Together

The neighborhood turned strange after the killings. Five bodies, impossible to identify, the weapon a mystery. Hank stopped smoking cigarettes on his front steps in the evening. Mathilde started wearing blouses that covered her midriff. Virginia slept with the radio on so loud we could all hear it. I'd swear the cats stopped slinking about at night, that the raccoons took their bandit eyes elsewhere. I still meditated each morning, but I felt the birds silently watching each breath. None of us wanted to turn off the lights. We'd hear it again, the voice: "Ready or not, here I come."

Usefulness

When Celeste slept, she sometimes spoke Portuguese, her mother's language, although she couldn't speak a word of it when awake. Her mother lived next to the Desert Casino now. Celeste played blackjack for hours when she visited. "We're always at the mercy of another one's dreams," her father told her just before he died. He'd probably planned to depart with a riddle. He wore a cape as a young man, and he claimed to know a necromancer. Guns fired at night in the distance. Pavilions of cacti harbored desiccated secrets. "Never stop, never now," a crooner sang in the bar.

Shirley Temple

I sat at the bar, my feet swinging from a stool. Jacksonville, 1972. The adults crowded into a circular booth in the corner. Men pinched women. Women squirmed in squirmy dresses. I smelled the chlorine on my hands as I listened to the cackles of laughter. My father told me I could have as many Shirley Temples as I wanted, but I drank slowly, counting to fifty before taking a single bird-like sip. The cherry bobbed slowly lower in the glass, almost dissolving like candy. I wouldn't eat it until it rested on the bottom. It's good to have rules.

John Cheever's Dinner Guest

Francine was the sort of woman who spoke in clichés, asked the price of everything. "What a charming setting," she said of the dining room. "That highboy was a nice purchase." When the conversation turned to the topic of travel, she seized the moment to tell about her time in Paris when she was eighteen. "There's nothing like Paris," she sighed. We joked later that she deserved to be stranded with a flat tire, get chased by a dog, marry a man with Tourrette Syndrome, something. She smiled at everyone she met, though, unlike us. We couldn't begrudge her that.

Letters from the Crypt

Gerard put all the items in a nondescript box: the letters, the journal Celeste had given him, the sticky notes with secret missives. He wrapped her collage in wax paper like an art curator would. The red swath of fingernail polish, images of a blindfolded woman. He'd written her a long letter interpreting the work, but he'd been beguiled by the woman, dainty yet waiting for a firing squad. Odd to archive torrents of emotions. Packing tape like a lock on an old mortuary. One never opens a crypt, yet the body is always primped and dressed for a ball.

Fatherhood

Quentin fingered the gold band of the once-ticking wristwatch and stared at its cracked face. He'd given the watch to Anton for his eighteenth birthday. A man needs a good watch, his father had told him. Life defined as keeping track of time. He wondered what had caused the face to crack. A fall on the ice. A fight in a bar. An argument with a girlfriend. A father wants to know his son, to feel at one with this creature he's put on the planet. What questions to ask? The facts of a life tend to hide its essence.

One Kind of Family

Kay would always think of sex as a catfight in the dark. Her father, Leopold, invested everything in a waterbed store in 1981. "It's the new thing," he said with a bluster that didn't fit his guttural accent. When asked where he came from, he always said, "Just west of paradise." The store failed. Leopold insisted they'd learn something valuable from their bad luck. Afterward, Kay had to sleep on the floor of a one-bedroom apartment. Her mother lay stiff, playing dead in the bed's swells. Leopold strained to the point of trembling. His green eyes so avid, forever determined.

Rings

Mathilde wore a ruby ring, given to her by her grandmother, who told her she possessed special powers and had to help people. One night, she walked by a baccarat table in a casino, and a chill seized her. A gambler's eyes needled her with frustration. She saw his head lying in blood. "Let me help you," she said. His hands caressed her like a teenager's, hungry and wanting. He breathed like a sprinter. He snuck out of the room without a word. She spotted his wedding ring, and slid it on her finger, just as she heard the scream.

Deluge

During Hurricane Sandy, Celeste picked up a man in a bar to help her get through the storm. They clung to each other under the covers as tree branches slapped the windows. His name was Clive. His breath tasted like menthol molasses. His eyebrows wiggled when he dreamed. Life is clinging, she thought. The next morning, Clive stood in his boxers in her kitchen, his spindly body showing more bone than muscle. The storm would've washed him away. "When are we getting married?" he asked. When she blew at him, his hair didn't move. He returned with only a toothbrush.

Skins

If only we could go out back, like when we were kids, and smoke and fool around. Our parents at parties, ashtrays filling up with butts, rumblings of laughter. There was always the question why they wanted us to grow up to be like them. They didn't imagine we'd mingle with evil. They didn't anticipate inclinations toward torpor. We thought the husbands loved the wives and vice versa, boxer shorts and JC Penney bras. But we knew better, mosquitoes biting our tender skin. We knew it's best to stay out of the way, even if there is no way back.

Three Sides

He was the unknown guest at a party who is introduced to no one. He watched families pull ice chests out of cars, open sodas, and traipse off to soccer games on irrigated fields. In a café, he listened to lovers deciding what movie to go to, where to dine. Clothes would drop to the floor that night, but they wouldn't be his. Drinking alone is so often disparaged, but each sip is like a meditator's breath. When the stripper moved his head between her breasts, he remembered how he'd liked studying triangles. Scalene, equilateral, isosceles, the lines always connected.

Touched

Del grew up in a brothel, so the word *whore* was no different to him than plumber or teacher. He watched his mom fasten her lacy underthings each morning and then put on a flower-print dress to take him to school. In the evenings, he'd see her out front, a cigarette dangling in her hand, her flesh white and soft in the moonlight. Men's eyes opened wide and eager when she talked to them. "Your mom's got a gift," one said to him. Del was the only man at her funeral. Somewhere, though, kisses still salved wounds in the darkness.

Correspondence

Celeste held the blank sheet of paper in her hand as if it were a razor blade. It arrived at her office in an envelope with no return address. A single sheet of ivory paper with rough edges, no writing on it. Fancy paper. She held it under water to see if invisible ink would materialize. Nothing. She hung it with a clothespin in the sunshine to dry. It whispered to her. She licked it. She lay with it on her breasts. She put it in an envelope and sent it to Gerard. Finally, after all the years, they'd spoken.

The End of the World Will Be Broadcast

Sometimes when Jeremiah looked up, he saw a hairline fracture in the sky. The way the world was falling apart held beauty if viewed right. Like peeling paint. The sky turned mustard green and passions rose with the fires and the top scientists in the world said on CNN, "We know now. We know now." Tombstone salesmen wished the world would fall apart at a pace that allowed just enough time for proper grieving. He sat on his porch staring through his opera glasses. He telephoned girls he'd gone to high school with and asked if he could kiss them.

Fear and Trembling

The clerk at the vitamin store sneaks a cigarette. My friend who works at Planned Parenthood has unprotected sex in airport bathrooms. I once heard a doctor ask, "What is health?" I'm reminded of Abraham holding a knife over his son, a sacrifice commanded by God. Faith? A monk burns himself in front of the White House. A skinny boy buys a gallon of protein powder. A virgin practices a sultry wink in the mirror. I look both ways when I cross the street. Each time my heartbeat skips, though, I wonder. A prayer, a scotch, a dare, a prayer.

The Sculptor

A sensation gripped Neva like one she used to feel long ago when, off for a swim, she prepared to plunge into the water. If Anna Karenina had owned a cell phone, Neva thought, she wouldn't have checked it for a text message at the train station. Life is suspension, the swaying of another's disregard. Aren't we all flung onto this earth to hate and torment each other, after all? Neva drew her head back into her shoulders and stretched her hands before her. The beginning of love always happens randomly, but endings can be shaped into exquisite, immortal perfection.

Climbing

We sat by the fire, everyone planning ways to change their lives. I couldn't count the number of times I'd planned such things, but I could count the number of times I'd succeeded. I drifted away, followed what looked like a path into the forest. The glow of the fire grew small, the voices scattered. I climbed a tree, just for the hell of it. I sat on a branch, too small for a man my size. As I looked up into the majestic whorls of stars in the sky, I dropped my last cigarette. You've arrived, an owl cooed.

The Gloaming

Somewhere a rooster crowed, a pig snuffled in the muddy street. The light of the oncoming jungle dawn soured the drunken light in the room. Someone said *wakan* was the Indian word for Great Mystery. A word that didn't apply to the man fumbling with his trousers at the bar, a hand upon fat Suzie's shoulders, as if touching a woman for the first time. Her rolling r's filled the room, a song. "Woo-man," the man called her. It always seemed like a possibility, to collide with the moon. When Suzie came back out, her lipstick and earrings were gone.

From There On

We went by mule or canoe. One end-of-the-road town, then another. We arrived in Toca late at night and drank a beer on the hotel's shabby veranda under the dubious gaze of a national cop who couldn't make up his mind to question us or not. Muddy streets. A light bulb dangled from a frayed wire. We asked for the medicine man, a wastrel whose payment was a bottle of whiskey. He soaked bark in cold water, sprinkled powders, giggled, then handed us the infusion in a palm leaf cup. "You'll see cities," he said. "Spiders will become your friends."

Nothing Is True,
Everything Is Permitted

by William S. Burroughs, May 2013

Sure, you think it's romantic, traipsing through the places of dead roads, calling partisans of all nations, eating the smoked pancreas of a two-toed sloth, trying to feel all of the ways you can feel. Could feel. It's all in a day's work. The Ugly Spirit fiddle-fucks the Navajo shaman who's telling which winds to sniff to find the final fix. Cut word lines— Shift linguals—Vibrate tourists—Free doorways—Break through Gray Room. Everything is true, nothing is permitted. Only the colorless no-smell of death. He do the police in different voices. If you can't be just, be arbitrary.

All the Foreigners

Where am I going in such a hurry? Appointment in Talara, Tingo Maria, Pucalpa, Panama, Mexico City? I don't know. I am alone in a nowhere place. The rotting smell of a viral stasis. I pound on the Peruvian consul's door so I can get a visa and leave a day early, all for the pains of a jarring bus ride. Three times "all the foreigners" have been asked to get out of the bus and register with the police. I'm the only one. Passport number, age, profession. My fellow passengers stare blankly, hoping I'll give them a little drama.

Who, If Anyone

The concoction of leaves seemed sacred. We considered several different titles for our masterpiece: "The Preparation," "The Murder of the Universe," "The Cure Sessions." It would never be completed, of course, but it was good to think so. The hut rayed with spectral presences, and I felt like a snake vomiting out the universe. "If any interplanetary news comes through," I said, "I'll relay it on the wires in a way it won't get fucked up." The holes in her t-shirt, the cigarette dangling from her lips. "I wish I knew who, if anyone, knows who I am," she said.

Wall Paintings

Jasper took out the penlight he'd stolen from Speedie's bag yesterday after they shot up. Irresistible. Life, a collection of trinkets. The beam of light floated on the stained yellow walls of the hotel room, walls painted by the cycles of moons in his primordial dreams. Somewhere there was a bison and a stag, a man lifting a bottle to his lips, a woman crying. His trick had left hours ago. His uncircumcised dick a scissor's blade. Their eyes had flickered with panic in what others would call love making. Hell cried out to heaven. Heaven cried out to hell.

Bras

The black bra lay on the bedroom floor, wadded up like a piece of litter. Gerard hugged Marie last night in the affectionate yet unerotic way he'd hug his mother. Years ago, just after college, he'd found a bra in a Laundromat dryer, a gaudy pink bra with black lace running along the edges, and he stole away with it, a sexual treasure, an accoutrement of masturbation. He'd touched few breasts at that point, and he'd only touch a few more before marriage. The black bra, a wilted plant. Its lace supported the gravity of flesh, but that was all.

The Art of It

That stale summer dawn smell in the garage. Warm rain on the iron roof. Morning light on cold coffee. These are things I know; I breathe in moments others pass by.

"Once a junkie, always spongy and rotten," my sister said.

"I prefer to think of it as a lifetime spent in research," I replied. "The algorithms of these bodily reactions don't come easy."

But there's no section on getting high on the SAT test. Only Tesla might understand my genius. Few have seen iridescent lagoons as I have. Few can sing with the hum of a refrigerator at midnight.

Looking In

From oil boomtown to oil boomtown we moved. Mud tents, rain barrels, struggle. On one side of the table was a huge lion, and in the chair on the other side was a huge tiger. They wouldn't let me participate. The thing inside, it was beautiful, kaleidoscopic in color. I told no one that I loved the clean-cut bodies of the Greeks. I was the kid with the mangy ears and biscuits sopped in syrup. My love for the gingerbread man, the cat staring at me with eyes as big as mill wheels. The smell of a box of watercolors.

This Great Thing

The blood was bad, they said, and the children were marked. My father shouldn't have married my mother because such blood would go for generations. A clot of the brain, insanity. "I'm worried about Forrest," my grandmother said. "He daydreams." I ran for my favorite place in the tall weeds, near the railroad tracks. Thousands of little nests swayed in the breeze, each containing the decaying body of a gull. You can't do anything but shake your head and cry because you don't comprehend this great thing. As wild as ocean currents. As fragile as pink wisps of a cloud.

First Time

Gerard sat next to the old woman at the hotel bar, staring at the soft creases around her eyes as if they were exotic etchings. She drank rye, "like my parents did," she said. Summers on Cape Cod. She insisted on turning out the lights when he unbuttoned her blouse. She ran her fingers over his chest as if touching a man for the first time. Nearing fifty, now he got to play the role of the younger man. Taut muscles. Years to live. He combed his fingers through her thin, white hair. "Do you believe in ghosts?" he asked.

Ooze

In another lifetime, Gerard and Celeste lived in a cottage made of thin boards above a small lake. Perhaps Portugal. Perhaps 1955. Each morning Gerard would put a bottle of wine in the water to cool, and they'd drink it at lunch, thinking of little more than the embroidered hems of waves on the shoreline. Snakes paused to watch them. Celeste smoked a cigarette, kissing puffs into Gerard's mouth. They observed the ways sand oozed between their toes, and she smoothed the tufts of hair on his eyebrows. The pumpkin-yellow glow of the sunset. Fireflies like sprites in the trees.

A Note from the Author

The story of any creation seems to rely on a smattering of random elements that somehow all come together.

I wouldn't have ever conceived of writing 100-word stories if I hadn't read Paul Strohm's 100-word pieces in *Eleven Eleven* one night (after clicking on a link on Facebook). And then I don't know if I would have had the persistence to go deeper into the form if I didn't work with publishing partners and friends Lynn Mundell and Beret Olsen to put out a journal dedicated to the form, *100 Word Story*. In fact, I thank all of the authors who contributed such amazing, arresting stories to *100 Word Story*, expanding my notion of what a 100-word story could be.

One thing leads to another. I'd been a writer who didn't share his work much, and certainly didn't read it in public, but this tiny form opened up big friendships with other writers in the flash fiction community. I've learned so much from writer friends Meg Pokrass, Jane Ciabatarri, Pamela Painter, Robert Scotellaro, and Thaisa Frank—and then all of the writers who have read at the fabulous Flash Fiction Collective readings.

Mainly, though, it's amazing that I've never had to wake up and justify my decision to be a writer to anyone. After spending all sorts of money to send me to college, my parents never questioned how I was going to make a living through storytelling. In fact, they did quite the opposite. They supported and celebrated this sometimes dubious aspiration, even when it was fraught with dead ends and meanderings that didn't have identifiable destinations.

Likewise, I can thank my rollicking and rambunctious family, which exists largely in the necessary mess of creativity (the dishes can always wait if a good story is on the line). The busy life of a working parent granted me accidental spaces to write stories in: between innings of baseball games, during the truncated daydreams before school performances, on the long drives to a soccer game. Heather, Jules, and Simone roam at the edges of all my writing, if not on top of it, in these small, noisy quarters that make for a big home.

GRANT FAULKNER likes big stories and small stories. He is the Executive Director of National Novel Writing Month and the co-founder of *100 Word Story*. His stories and essays have appeared in *The New York Times*, *Poets & Writers*, *Writer's Digest*, *The Southwest Review*, *PANK*, *Gargoyle*, *eclectica*, *Puerto del Sol*, the *Berkeley Fiction Review*, and *Word Riot*, among many others. He lives in Berkeley with a family of writers and a dog that insists on sitting on his lap each morning when he writes.

www.ingramcontent.com/pod-product-compliance
Lightning Source LLC
Chambersburg PA
CBHW020647250626
47154CB00008B/2848